RANGER in TIME

escue on the Oregon Trail

KATE MESSNER

illustrated by
KELLEY McMORRIS

Scholastic Inc.

For Jamie and Tracy
(and all the dogs they've loved)

Text copyright © 2015 by Kate Messner
Illustrations copyright © 2015 by Scholastic Inc.

This book is being published simultaneously in hardcover by Scholastic Press.

Library of Congress Cataloging-in-Publication Data
Messner, Kate, author.
Rescue on the Oregon trail / Kate Messner. — First edition.
pages cm. — (Ranger in time)
Summary: Ranger, a golden retriever, could have been a great search-and-rescue-dog except for the squirrels — but one day he unearths a mysterious box and finds himself transported back to the year 1850 where his faithful service is really needed by a family traveling west along the Oregon Trail.
1. Golden retriever — Juvenile fiction. 2. Working dogs — Juvenile fiction. 3. Time travel — Juvenile fiction. 4. Adventure stories. 5. Oregon National Historic Trail — Juvenile fiction. 6. West (U.S.) — History — 1848-1860 — Juvenile fiction. [1. Golden retriever — Fiction. 2. Working dogs — Fiction. 3. Dogs — Fiction. 4. Time travel — Fiction. 5. Adventure and adventurers — Fiction. 6. Oregon National Historic Trail — Fiction. 7. West (U.S.) — History — 1848-1860 — Fiction.] I. Title.
PZ10.3.M5635Re 2015
813.6 — dc23 2014005485

ISBN 978-0-545-63914-9

10 9 8 7 6 5 4 3 2 1   15 16 17 18 19/0

Printed in the United States of America   40
First printing 2015

Book design by Ellen Duda

Chapter 1

SEVENTY-FIVE POUNDS OF BACON

Sam Abbott lugged another sack of bacon to the wagon and sat down to wipe his forehead.

"Two more to go!" Pa swung the bacon into place beside a barrel of flour. "Mr. Palmer says we need seventy-five pounds for each adult."

"Too bad Mr. Palmer isn't here to help us carry it," Sam said.

Mr. Palmer had written the guidebook their father held as close as the Bible these days. It told the story of his trip to the Oregon Territory and gave suggestions for how other folks could make the same journey to the fresh air and

1

rich farmland of the Willamette Valley. Most, like Sam's family, traveled to Independence, Missouri, or one of the other jumping-off points first. There, they could get supplies and meet up with a wagon train. Traveling together was safer. For each adult on the journey, Mr. Palmer said to pack:

200 pounds of flour

75 pounds of bacon

30 pounds of pilot bread

10 pounds of rice

Sam and his father had packed some of that before the family set out from their farm near Boonville, Missouri, six days ago. When they arrived in Independence, they'd purchased

the rest at a busy trading post. Now they had to finish loading it into the wagon.

Sam's arms ached. How was he going to make it two thousand miles to Oregon when he was already tuckered out just from loading supplies?

And how was he going to make it without Scout? They'd left their farm hound behind in Boonville with Uncle Jim and Aunt Cecelia. Pa said poor Scout was too old to come so far. He said it wouldn't be fair. Sam didn't think it was fair to make *him* go, either. But nobody seemed to care about that. They were setting out on the trail this morning, now that the grass had grown enough for the oxen and horses to eat along the route.

"Sam, are you looking after Amelia?" his mother called from the wagon. She and Sam's older sister, Lizzie, were packing herbs and medicine into a small wooden chest.

"She's here, playing with Mabel and Peg." Sam slid off the back of the wagon and shuffled past his three-year-old sister. Amelia was making her rag doll dance for the chickens they'd brought to lay eggs along the way.

Sam was about to grab another sack of bacon when he heard a shout.

"Whoa!"

A horse had broken away from its owner and was tearing through the square. It reared up every time someone snatched at its reins. It raced this way and that, kicking up dust and knocking over barrels. Finally, the owner got it tied up to a post and turned his attention to an auction happening by the courthouse.

"Twenty dollars!"

"Twenty there! Do I hear twenty-five now? Twenty-five? He's a fine, strong mule, gentlemen."

"Twenty-five!"

Independence was full of travelers passing through. Some, like Sam's family, were making the trip to the Oregon Territory for better farmland. Others were going to California to search for gold. When some of them heard stories about disease, starvation, and snowstorms along the route, they decided they weren't up for the trip after all. Then they started auctioning off their mules to the highest bidders.

Sam sat down on a heap of sacks and watched. He wondered what it would be like to set off on his own to find gold in a mountain stream.

"Sam!" Pa called from the wagon. "We can't eat your daydreams out on the trail. Load the rest of that bacon!"

Sam stood up and sighed. He shoved a hand into his pocket and felt the folded-up friendship quilt squares his cousins had made. They hadn't finished in time to include them in the big quilt that Aunt Cecelia put together for their family, but they gave them to Sam anyway. He was glad. He liked having three small squares of home in his pocket. One had a picture of Scout, carefully outlined in thread. Another square showed the crooked apple tree by the fence. The third showed the Abbotts' farmhouse and barn, pieced together with colorful scraps of fabric. Sam already missed home so much.

Pa said it was all right to be sad. "But your heart has room to love more than one place," he'd promised. Pa said the Oregon Territory was a land of milk and honey. He said it would be one of those places to love for sure. Still, Sam couldn't help worrying it would be like Independence — a land of dust, smelly animals, and stale bread.

At least they'd have bacon. He hugged another sack to his chest.

"Amelia!" Sam's mother called out. She was searching around the wagon frantically. "Amelia!" Her eyes landed on Sam. "Where is she?"

"I was watching her, but . . ." Sam ran to where his sister had been. Her doll lay in the dirt next to the chicken coop. Sam picked it up and looked around.

Amelia was gone.

Chapter 2

MYSTERY IN THE GARDEN

"Whatcha got, Ranger? What did you find, boy?" Luke called from the porch swing where he and Sadie were finishing their pizza slices for lunch.

Ranger was too busy digging in the garden to look up. Ranger loved to dig. He loved the damp smell of earth. He loved the showers of dirt and rock that flew from under his paws and pattered on the ground behind him. He loved finding things — especially bones!

There was something hard buried here.

Ranger wasn't sure if it was a bone. He lowered his head to sniff the thing.

Not a bone.

Metal. It smelled old.

He sniffed again, and caught another scent on the wind.

Squirrel!

Ranger whipped his head around.

There! By the picnic table!

Ranger took off running, and so did the squirrel. It was fast, but Ranger was bigger, and he was catching up.

Ranger loved chasing squirrels. He'd never caught one. He wasn't sure what he would do if he did. But they were such fun to chase with their twitchy, fluffy tails. He chased it twice around the picnic table. Over a bench. Around the birdbath.

As Ranger was getting close, the squirrel

raced up an oak tree. It perched on a way-up branch and chattered down at him.

Sadie laughed. "Another one got away!"

"Poor Ranger. You still can't resist those squirrels, can you?" Luke came over and scratched Ranger's ear. "You would have been such a good search-and-rescue dog."

Ranger thought so, too. He pushed his head into Luke's fingers.

Squirrels were the reason Ranger couldn't be a search-and-rescue dog.

Ranger had done all the training with Luke and Dad. They went to a special school with other dogs — German shepherds and Labradors and other golden retrievers like Ranger. There, they learned to rescue people in trouble.

When Luke ran into the woods and hid, Ranger could always find him. He knew to stay there and bark until Dad came. That's what you did with lost people. You had to stay with them and signal an alert to bring help.

Ranger had practiced finding Luke in all different situations. He'd practiced finding other people, too. He could sniff a person's shirt or hat and then follow the smell of that person in the air to wherever the person had gone. Ranger was *excellent* at sniffing and finding.

But to be a search-and-rescue dog, you had to ignore squirrels. Even when they raced right past you, flicking their fluffy tails. You weren't allowed to take off and chase them. You had to pretend the squirrels weren't even there.

But they were! So Ranger chased them every time. He couldn't resist.

Why was that a problem? It was only practice, after all. Ranger would never go chasing after a squirrel if a real, live person needed help.

But the man who worked with Luke and

Dad couldn't seem to understand. "I'm sorry," he told them. "I just can't pass him."

Luke had looked sad about that. It made Ranger sad for a moment, too. But then a squirrel had come flying across the lawn, and Ranger chased it all around in circles. That made him feel much better.

That squirrel had gotten away, just like this one in the yard. It was way up in the tree now.

Sadie and Luke went inside to take care of their pizza plates, so Ranger went back to the garden to dig. Soon, he had the metal thing uncovered. It was a box with a strap made from some kind of animal hide. Ranger clamped his teeth onto the leather and tugged the box from the hole. It had symbols like the ones Ranger had seen on a smaller white box in a cabinet inside the house.

FIRST AID

Ranger sniffed the box. It didn't smell like there were bones inside. He would have to dig some more and keep looking. But as Ranger turned back toward the garden, he heard a high-pitched humming sound.

His ears twitched. It was coming from the box.

He sniffed the metal. Vibrations tickled his nose. What was *in* there?

If Ranger took the box to Luke, he could open it and they could find out.

The box was too big for Ranger to hold in his mouth, so he poked his nose under the leather strap and nuzzled it over his head. When he lifted the box from the dirt, the humming got louder.

The box felt warm at Ranger's throat. Bright light spilled from cracks in the old metal and seemed to swallow up the whole yard.

Ranger's skin prickled under his fur. The

light coming from the box grew brighter and brighter. The metal rattled and shook. Ranger whimpered.

He flopped down in the grass and tried to paw the box away, but all he could see was white-hot light. *Too bright!* The light spread and grew. There was a blinding flash, and Ranger felt as if he were being squeezed through a hole in the sky. He closed his eyes until the humming stopped and the hot metal cooled.

When he opened them, he found himself on a dusty road crowded with people. They weren't dressed like Ranger's family. The men and boys wore long pants and button-up shirts. The girls had skirts and aprons like the kind Sadie wore when she played dress-up.

Ranger sniffed the air. This was not his backyard.

He smelled campfires and horses and chickens. He smelled coffee and hot grease . . . and
bacon! But above it all, he smelled men. Crowds
of them, hurrying and carrying and loading.
They smelled of dust and smoke and sweat.

Ranger pricked up his ears. This wasn't
Luke's neighborhood. There were no shouting
playground voices, no zooming cars. Instead,
hooves clopped and thumped the unpaved
streets. Animals whinnied and neighed and
snorted. Men shouted at one another across
the busy square.

"Get up, Fergus! Haw!"

"Hurry now!"

"Deal of a lifetime on two yoke of oxen!"

Then Ranger heard a woman's voice, shrill
and full of fear. He didn't know who she was,
but he understood her frantic words. "Find
her! Find her now!"

Chapter 3

TROUBLE IN THE TOWN SQUARE

Ranger didn't recognize this place. He didn't know where he was. But he knew how to find.

He'd practiced with Luke and Dad over and over. They'd hold out an old shirt or hat and say, "*Find* that! Find it, Ranger!"

First, Ranger would smell the thing. Sometimes, it smelled like rain or dirt or other things. But it would always smell like a person, too.

Once Ranger knew that *person* smell, he could find it anywhere. Even if there were a thousand other smells to sort through, Ranger could pick out the important one and follow it until he found the person.

When he did, Luke would scratch Ranger's ears and say, "Good dog! Good boy!" And then they would go home.

Home. Ranger sniffed the dusty air. Where was Luke? Maybe if he did his work, if he found the person, Luke would come and say, "Good job!" and they could go home.

Ranger trotted up to the woman to see what she wanted him to find.

Her eyes were wet. Ranger nuzzled her hand, but she waved him away. "Go on, dog!" She didn't offer him anything to smell. She just ran off, calling, "Amelia! Amelia!"

But then a boy came. He looked about as old as Luke, with longer hair, and he held something in his hand. Ranger sniffed at it.

The boy held it out. It was a little cloth person, like the ones Sadie played with at home. The ones Luke liked to hide from her.

"This is Amelia's doll." The boy sighed.

Ranger sniffed the doll all over. He could smell smoke and dirt and another dog. But mostly he could smell *person*. Was it the person Ranger was supposed to find? He sniffed again. Then he looked up at the boy.

"You smell her?" The boy looked at Ranger with frantic eyes. "I've got to find her!"

Find! Ranger could do that. He tipped his head and waited for the boy to put on his harness the way Dad and Luke did. But the boy just stood there.

So Ranger sniffed the air and started walking. He paused and looked back at the boy, who was still standing in the same spot. Luke and Dad always followed him. Ranger barked.

"What is it?" the boy asked. "You want me to come with you? Can you find her?"

Find!

Ranger barked again.

The boy ran to catch up, and together they weaved through the busy crowds.

The street here wasn't hard and smooth like at home — it was loose and dusty under Ranger's paws. And the cars here didn't roar or zoom. They had bigger wheels. Huge, drooling animals tugged them along.

"Amelia!" the boy shouted. But Ranger hadn't found her smell.

"Maybe over here." The boy headed toward a noisy building with horses and men crowded outside. As they got closer, Ranger's nose filled with a thousand scents.

Horses! Men!

Shaggy animal!

Bacon! Chickens! Smoke!

And then . . . that!

Ranger stopped and sniffed. It was the Amelia smell!

He ran in a circle, found where the scent was strongest, and followed it. But the boy said, "Uh-oh!" and stopped.

Ranger pricked up his ears. Angry voices filled the air. Ahead of them, two sweaty men circled each other, shouting. One shoved the other so hard he flew backward into one of the horses. It neighed and reared up. The other horses and mules fretted and stomped the dirt.

The man who had fallen got up and ran at the other man. The crowd was getting thicker. Tense voices buzzed in the hot afternoon air. It made the fur on Ranger's neck prickle.

The boy must have felt the trouble, too. "Come on, dog," he whispered. "We better go. She's not here."

But she *was*! The Amelia smell was getting stronger. Ranger kept going, into the thick of the crowd, without checking to see if the boy had followed.

One of the angry men lunged at the other, and Ranger had to leap out of their way, but he kept going, kept smelling, and finally . . .

There!

A tiny girl stood in the center of the mob. She toddled close to one of the shaggy animals and reached up for its whip of a tail.

Ranger barked. He looked for the boy and barked again.

There was a shout, then a gasp from the crowd.

Horses neighed. Hooves thundered. Voices hollered, "Whoa!"

And the square exploded into a swirling cloud of dust.

Chapter 4

WAGON TRAIN WEST

"Amelia!" Sam caught only a glimpse of his sister before it happened.

She was across the square next to one of the oxen. The dog was there, too, barking like crazy.

But the moment Sam stepped into the square, one of the men tackled the other, and they rolled through the dust. It was all too much for the nervous horses. One reared up and then another, and the next thing Sam knew, a yoke of oxen had broken free, and the beasts were racing toward him.

"Watch out, son!" A rough hand closed around his arm and yanked him out of the way just as the oxen thundered past. When they were gone, the man let go of Sam's arm and shook his head. "Those young men from St. Louis are nothin' but trouble. They got gold fever, and it's turned them into a pack of fools."

Sam could only stare as the men in the square rushed after runaway oxen and terrified horses. He looked across to where he'd seen his sister, but she was gone.

Without thanking the man or saying goodbye, Sam took off across the square.

"Amelia!"

She didn't answer. People were staring at Sam now, but he didn't care. He swiped tears from his eyes with his shirtsleeve, then stood in the center of the square, searching. He couldn't see her anywhere.

Sam felt a hand on his arm. "Do you need help?" He turned and saw a girl about his age. Her eyes were full of concern. "Who's Amelia?"

"My sister," Sam said. "I was supposed to be watching her, and —"

"I'll help you look," the girl said, pushing through the crowd.

"Amelia!" Sam called, even louder. It was hopeless. Even if she answered, he'd never be able to hear in all this chaos.

But then he heard a bark.

Sam whirled around toward the sound, and there, tucked into the blacksmith's doorway, was the dusty golden dog, standing guard over Amelia. No . . . not standing guard so much as holding her prisoner. Every time Amelia tried to toddle back into the busy square, the dog moved to block her way.

Sam ran over and scooped his sister up in his arms. "We found you!"

"That doggie did," she said, looking down at the dog slobber on her skirt. "He pushed me over here."

The older girl gave the dog a pat. "Good dog!"

"Thanks for offering to help me," Sam told her.

"It was no trouble. I have plenty of experience tracking down little runaways." She smiled at Amelia.

"You have sisters, too?"

The girl shook her head. "Mother and Father wanted a big family but only got me. I have lots of cousins that I help look after, though. They've already gone west, and we're joining them now. I'm Sarah Ferguson, by the way."

"Sam Abbott." He shook her hand. "We're off to the Oregon Territory. My Uncle Thomas and his family went out last year."

Amelia squirmed, so Sam put her down but kept a tight grip on her hand. The dog stayed close to her, too. "Maybe you should come with us, dog. You're better at watching Amelia than I am."

Ranger barked and licked Sam's hand.

Sarah laughed. "He'd make a fine nurse-maid. I'd better get back to my parents. I hope I'll see you on the trail." She waved and hurried off toward the wagons.

Sam bent down to scratch behind the dog's ear, then touched the metal box Ranger carried. "What's that?" Sam lifted it from around Ranger's neck, opened it up, and looked at the bandages and vials tucked inside. "You carrying these supplies for someone?" Sam looked around. "Where's your owner, dog?"

Ranger tipped his head. Where *was* Luke? Ranger had found the person. Wasn't it time to go home?

But then Ranger remembered back to one of his last training sessions. He'd found Luke hiding in an old barrel and was ready to get his ears scratched and go home. But Dad waved a baseball hat and said, "Find *more!*" Ranger had to keep searching until he found Luke's friend Will behind a big box. Sometimes, more than one person needed to be found.

Could this be one of those times?

"You're lost, aren't you?" Sam looked the dog over. "Maybe you really can come with us!"

Ranger didn't know what else to do, so he followed Sam and little Amelia back to the Abbotts' wagon. The person called Ma gave Ranger a grumpy look at first. But when Sam told her what happened, she softened and tossed Ranger a scrap of bacon.

It was greasy and salty and good.

Sam had a bigger family than Luke. Besides his little sister, Amelia, and their parents, Sam had a big sister named Lizzie and a baby brother named Isaac who rode around in Ma's arms most of the time. Amelia was always trying to wander, though. Ranger stayed close to her while the rest of the family packed barrels and crates. They tucked Ranger's metal box from the garden alongside some tools and even loaded the chicken coop onto their wagon. When it was full and the big animals were attached to the front, Sam knelt down in the dirt next to Ranger.

"You're coming with us, right? Right, boy?"

Ranger looked around for Luke. Where *was* he?

Sam scratched Ranger behind his ear and stood up. "It's time to head out on the trail."

Ranger looked for Luke again. He couldn't

find him. But he saw the little Amelia girl tugging away from her big sister's hand, trying to run off. Ranger decided he needed to help look after her "out on the trail," wherever that was. Sam was going. It looked like all the bacon was going. Maybe Luke would be there, too.

So when the Abbott family left Independence, Missouri, that morning, Ranger followed their wagon down the well-worn path out of town.

Chapter 5

MILES AND MILES AND
BUFFALO DUNG

"Get on now, Fergus! Get on, Jed!"

Pa hollered to the oxen from his horse. He and the other men rode their horses alongside the teams of oxen to keep them moving. Sam wished he were older so he could help, but all he could do was walk with Lizzie and Ma and the other women and children. Amelia rode in the wagon most of the time. When she did get out to walk, the new dog stayed close and nudged her every time she slowed down.

"You're like a sheepdog, rounding everybody up." Sam reached down to pet Ranger's head. "I wish I knew your name. I guess you can just be Dog for now."

"I am amazed that you convinced your father to keep him," Ma said. But Sam had seen Pa looking back at the farm when they'd pulled out of Boonville a week ago. They had heard Scout barking all the way down the road. Pa's eyes had been just as shiny and wet as Sam's. He missed Scout, too.

Sam looked over his shoulder. An endless train of wagons stretched out behind them, all heading west. "I sure hope the Willamette Valley has as much land as they say. I don't think anyone's going to be left back east."

"We could still turn around," Lizzie said, scuffing her boots in the dust. "Let everyone else run off to be taken ill and attacked by Indians."

"We'll be just fine, Lizzie," Ma said, but she started humming a hymn from church. She did that when she felt anxious, Sam knew. With such a long list of bad things that could happen out on the trail, she was humming a lot these days.

"Mr. Palmer says most of the Indians are friendly and just want to trade," Sam said. "He says some help with river crossings."

"Well, that's good," Ma said, and her humming quieted down. Ma and Pa trusted Mr. Palmer's book.

The guidebook also said that traveling in groups made the journey safer, and there were twenty wagons in the Abbotts' train. Sam's family and nine others were from Missouri, all hoping to settle on better farmland out west. The Harrigans and Middletons from Iowa had the same goal, along with Dr. Loring and his wife, plus six other families from Indiana. Sarah Ferguson and her parents were part of the wagon train, too. They were traveling from a place called Nauvoo, Illinois, to the Great Salt Lake where there was a much bigger community of Mormon families, including all those cousins Sarah was so good at chasing. For now, though, Sarah spent her time helping with Amelia, and Mrs. Abbott was happy to have another older child keeping watch.

Some of the men traveling alone hadn't bothered with wagons. Henry and Ezra Beard, brothers from St. Louis, only had mules. They were going to California to find gold.

When it was almost time for supper, the Beard brothers rode ahead to find a camping place. When everyone else arrived, all twenty wagons pulled into a circle for the night.

"Not bad for the first day. Seventeen miles!" Mr. Ferguson called out to the group.

The Fergusons had something called a roadometer attached to their wagon. It used cogs and gears to record the number of times the wagon wheels went around, and then turned that number to miles. Sarah told Sam it was invented a few years ago by a couple of Mormon pioneers who got tired of counting the wagon wheel rotations to measure distance.

"Can you imagine? They tied a rag to the wheel to make it easier to count rotations," she said. "Three hundred sixty turns made a mile."

"Probably helped pass the time," Sam said, reaching down to scratch Ranger's ear. There wasn't much else to do while you walked along with the wagon. He was glad they were done traveling for the day.

Pa unyoked the oxen for the night, and Ma let the chickens out to peck for bugs and worms in the grass. Sam and Sarah and the other children gathered wood for the fires. Then the women cooked up beans and bacon and trail bread for supper.

It had been such a long day of walking that Sam went right to sleep, even though his bed was just a couple blankets spread under the wagon. He drifted off to the sound of the horses chewing and fussing, Mr. Harrigan playing his fiddle a few wagons down, and Ranger snoring softly beside him.

In the morning, they had breakfast, loaded the wagons, hitched up the teams of oxen, and started off again. It wasn't a fast walk, but it was long. They only stopped once during the day, at noontime. Sometimes, Sam ran ahead with Amelia and Sarah and helped them pick flowers for Ma and Mrs. Ferguson.

Lizzie spent most of her time complaining. It was always too cold or too warm or too dusty. It was never home. Sam understood that. He missed the farm and his relatives who'd stayed behind in Boonville. He missed Scout, but he was glad this new dog had decided to come along. It was good to have furry company, especially with Lizzie being so cranky.

They made twenty miles the second day. Eighteen on the third. Just twelve the next day because they had to wait to ferry across a stream. With so many wagons heading west, it was hours before the Abbotts had their turn.

It was the longest walk Ranger had ever been on. Like going with Luke and Sadie to the park and home over and over and over without ever stopping to chase balls.

Where *was* Luke? Ranger looked for him every time the Abbotts pulled into camp for the night and every morning before they started out again. There were so many voices — so many faces — but none of them belonged to Luke.

As the days went by, everyone traveled more slowly. People got sick. Some of them got better, but not all. The smell of newly turned dirt made Ranger's fur stand up each time they passed a fresh grave.

The landscape changed, too. The earth was rough and sandy now, and the oxen's feet were swollen and cracked. The dust and rocks hurt Ranger's paws, too, but at least he had plenty of scraps to eat. The oxen were struggling to find enough grass.

"Poor Fergus and Jed," Sam said. "The buffalo out here have eaten up all the grass."

When they'd left Independence the second week of May, there were plenty of trees along the way. Now, wood was scarce. The women had started bringing back buffalo dung for the fires instead. Buffalo chips made a fine, clean fire. They were easy to find, but no one in the Abbotts' wagon train had seen an actual buffalo.

At first, Lizzie said she'd never eat anything cooked over buffalo chips, but that didn't last long. Lizzie was as hungry as anyone else after a day of walking.

. . .

One night in early June, the Abbotts made camp along Little Blue River. Sam was watching Amelia alone. Sarah's father wasn't feeling well, so she was busy helping her mother care for him. Lizzie and Ma had just come back to the wagon with their aprons full of buffalo chips when Sam thought he heard a rumbling. There were often thunderstorms on the prairie. He looked west, expecting to see storm clouds.

But the sky was as blue as could be.

"You hear that?" Sam asked Ranger.

Ranger not only heard it; he *felt* it in his paws. The rumbling was shaking the ground. He pawed at the dirt and pricked up his ears.

"You do hear, don't you, boy?" Sam squatted down next to Ranger. "What is it, Dog?"

Ranger whined. He sat up straight and sniffed the air.

Amid the dust and oxen and people smells, there was something new.

Animal smell.

Big animal smell.

Ranger tipped his head and barked. *There!*

He barked again and again.

Sam tried to pet him. "It's all right, Dog. That thunder's far away."

But Ranger pulled away and ran in circles, jumping and barking. Then he came back and pawed at Sam's leg.

"What is it, boy? What's wrong?" It reminded Sam of the time Scout had gone crazy, barking and jumping when their old barn caught fire. Scout had realized before anyone else that something was wrong.

"Pa!" Sam called. "Come quick!"

Pa hurried over, and Ranger jumped right

up on him. "What in heaven's name is the matter, Dog?" Ranger barked, then turned to the river. Pa stared across the water to the plains on the other side, and his eyes grew wide. He whirled around to Sam. "Find your sisters and get in the wagon. Hurry!"

Then Pa turned to the rest of the men. He hollered at the top of his voice, "Circle the wagons! The buffalo are coming!"

Chapter 6

STAMPEDE!

The buffalo were not only coming. They were thundering over the plains, heading for the river. If they crossed, they'd come ashore on top of the Abbotts' camp. The cattle were already fretting, stomping the dirt. The oxen tugged at their yokes.

"Amelia!" Sam called. He found her playing with a pan of bread dough Ma had set out to rise. Sam scooped her up in his arms and called to Lizzie, who was piling buffalo chips for the fire. "Leave that and come to the wagon, Pa says. There's buffalo coming!"

Pa and the other men drew the wagons and livestock together. They hurried the women and children into the wagons, then took their guns and ducked behind some rocks to wait. Ma held Baby Isaac close in one arm and circled the other tightly around Amelia. Ranger stayed close to her, too.

Lizzie leaned out the tailgate. "Won't they stop at the river?"

Sam climbed over the trunks and barrels to look. The buffalo didn't stop. They stampeded over the open land, down to the riverbank, and plunged in, one after another. The water churned and frothed into a boiling mud stew as the animals crossed.

Soon, the first beasts were climbing ashore, barreling toward the camp. They sounded like a great whooshing wind, like a storm blowing through. But instead of rain, the air was full of dust.

"Oh, Lord, keep us safe," Ma whispered, and started humming her worry-hymn. Pa and Mr. Harrigan fired their guns from behind the rocks, shooting into the stampede to try to scare the animals off their course. Pa's guidebook said that might work. If it didn't, Sam knew the whole camp could be destroyed. Henry and Ezra Beard stood side by side, firing into the herd. But the buffalo kept coming, as if they were covered in armor.

Sam watched from the wagon. His heart thumped along with all those pounding hooves in the dirt. Every time one of the men's guns exploded, Sam's breath caught in his throat.

Turn, turn! He willed the buffalo to change course. If they didn't, they'd stomp the wagons into splinters.

Turn!

Pa fired his rifle again and again. Finally, one of the buffalo stumbled and sank to the ground. The herd kept going, but the mass of animals veered away from the blast of the guns.

Sam felt a hot breeze as they rushed past, trampling the dry grass.

When the last of the herd had thundered off into the dust, Henry Beard let out a whoop. Pa and the other men jumped from the rocks. They ran toward the buffalo they'd taken down.

Sam climbed down from the wagon bed. He slapped his thighs. "Come on, Dog! Let's go see what they got!"

"Take this to your father." Ma handed Pa's big hunting knife down to Sam. "Be careful."

Ranger leaped from the wagon and kept close to Sam. There had been so many huge animals. The air was still full of their smell.

Ranger followed Sam up to the collapsed buffalo. Its legs were crumpled underneath its great body. Its fur was matted with dust and blood.

Mr. Harrigan and some of the gold rush boys from Missouri turned the buffalo over to expose its soft belly.

"We'll eat well tonight!" Pa said. He bent down to pat Ranger's head. "You heard them coming, didn't you, Dog? Good thing you let loose barking when you did."

Sam handed Pa his knife, and Pa slit the buffalo's hide from its throat all the way to its tail. Sam had to turn away. But later, after the sun had set and campfire smoke rose up into the clouds, he breathed in the greasy goodness of buffalo steaks sizzling over the fire. It was the first fresh meat they'd had since they set out from Independence.

"This is a little bit of heaven," Ma said as she bit into the steak.

"It's not very tender," Lizzie complained.

But she ate every last bite of the sweet, dark meat on her tin plate.

Sam finished his supper, too, and leaned back to look at the stars. He could hear the oxen and horses snorting and shuffling. It had taken them a while to settle down. He could hear Mr. Harrigan tuning his fiddle. He could hear Pa and the Beard brothers laughing as they told the story of bringing the buffalo down. Sam reached into his pocket and pulled out the quilt squares with the farmhouse and apple tree and Scout. What stories he'd have to write in his letters to everyone back home!

Sam's belly was full and warm. His eyes were drooping when Sarah came running across the circle to their fire, in tears. "Can you help me find Dr. Loring?"

Find? Ranger's ears pricked up.

Ma was already on her feet. "I think he had supper with the Middletons. Is it your father,

Sarah?" Mr. Ferguson had been sick for two days now.

Sarah nodded and let out a sob. "And Ma, too, now. It's bad. Oh, please! Come quick!"

Chapter 7

A SAD GOOD-BYE

Sam found Dr. Loring and brought him to Sarah's wagon. Dr. Loring climbed up to check on her parents, but it wasn't long before he returned.

"It's the cholera. I'm afraid they're both too far gone," Dr. Loring whispered to Ma so Sarah couldn't hear.

But Sam heard. His eyes stung with tears, and his throat got tight. The guidebooks all warned this trip was dangerous, and Sam knew that plenty of folks died out on the trail. But until now, they'd been nameless strangers — not people with actual voices and faces and hands Sam had shaken.

Dr. Loring sat beside Mr. and Mrs. Ferguson all night long. Sam and Ma stayed up with Sarah, worrying and wondering.

Ranger stayed, too, curled up next to Sarah by the campfire. He leaned his big, warm body against her. Ranger understood sad. He remembered when Luke and Sadie's grand-mother had died, and everyone cried. He understood there wasn't much you could do about sad. But snuggling sometimes helped a little, so that's what Ranger did.

In the morning, Dr. Loring came to the Abbotts' wagon. Sarah jumped up and started toward him. Dr. Loring shook his head. "I'm sorry," he said. "I'm so very sorry."

Sam watched Pa and Mr. Harrigan and the Beard brothers dig a grave for Mr. and Mrs. Ferguson. Ma tried to keep Sarah away, but she insisted on watching, too. She never cried. But Sam heard her whispering numbers. She counted every spadeful of dirt — all the way up to 237. She watched as they laid her mother and father down in the prairie, said some prayers, and shoveled all that dirt back in.

And then it was time to go. Sam felt like there should be more ceremony, more prayers, more time. But there were miles to be covered. They had to get through the mountains before winter.

So Pa hitched up the oxen. He shouted, "Get on, Fergus! Get on, Jed!" like he did every morning. The men drove every last wagon over the grave as if they were saying good-bye, but Sam knew the real reason. He'd heard the men talking about wolves. Running the wagons over the grave packed the earth so it was more likely Mr. and Mrs. Ferguson would rest in peace.

Sarah walked beside Sam and Ranger. She was part of the Abbott family for now. Ma had promised to take care of her until they got to the parting of the ways, where the trails split. There, Sarah's parents had planned to take the Mormon Trail to the Salt Lake Valley, where her Uncle Aaron and Aunt Helen and all those cousins were waiting to help them settle a new farm. When the Abbotts got to the next fort, Ma planned to send a message to Sarah's relatives so they could come meet them and take Sarah to her new home by the Great Salt Lake.

Every day that passed put more miles between Sarah and her parents' grave. She collected buffalo chips with Sam and Lizzie for the campfire each night, but she was quiet, as if part of her had died, too. Only the prairie dogs made her smile.

"They're curious creatures, aren't they?" Lizzie watched with Sarah as one little fellow peeked out of his hole. "Half squirrel and half puppy dog."

Ranger liked the prairie dogs, too. They'd stand at the openings to their burrows, barking as the wagons approached. Prairie dogs weren't as much fun as the squirrels at Luke's house, though. Squirrels raced around the yard and over the picnic table and zigzagged through the garden. Prairie dogs jumped into their holes and vanished as soon as Ranger came near.

Still, Ranger couldn't resist chasing a few along the way. He never got so carried away that he lost sight of Amelia, though. He stayed close to all the children when the wagon train crossed creeks in the daytime. He kept track of them when the wagons circled at night.

Ranger had come to love Sam and the rest of the Abbotts and Sarah, but he never stopped missing his *home* family. Each night, before he went to sleep, Ranger took a walk through the wagons, sniffing the evening air. He'd smell oxen and horses and simmering stew but never what he hoped for most. Because Luke wasn't there.

. . .

Each morning meant the start of another long walk. Sam tracked every mile in his father's guidebook. He looked forward to the land-marks Mr. Palmer had promised along the way. When Chimney Rock came into view, Sam nudged Sarah and pointed. "It's just as Mr. Palmer said! Like a haystack with a pole stick-ing out the top."

Sarah nodded, but she didn't smile. Sam had thought seeing the famous Chimney Rock might make her happier. It was a sign they were getting closer to their new home. But when Sam thought about it, he understood.

He couldn't imagine settling into a new home without Ma and Pa.

Four days later, the Abbotts and the rest of their wagon train arrived at Fort Laramie, a supply post about one third of the way to the Oregon Territory. They'd traveled more than six hundred miles from Missouri, but the flurry of activity reminded Sam of Independence all over again. The air was alive with excited voices and the clang of hammers as the blacksmith went about shoeing horses and oxen. There must have been two hundred wagons, along with Lakota Sioux men who had come on horses to trade. Travelers could buy flour, coffee, sugar, tobacco, powder, and lead at the fort.

The Abbotts and the rest of their wagon train only camped near the fort one night. Ma sent her message off to Sarah's aunt and uncle, and they started out again in the morning.

After Fort Laramie, there was another river crossing. It was deeper and faster than the others had been. Pa thought they could make it, but Ma shook her head. "This current's too fast. It's dangerous," she said. So Pa paid five dollars to have each wagon crossed over on a ferryboat.

Sam, Sarah, Lizzie, Ma, Amelia, and Baby Isaac rode in canoes with Lakota men. Ranger came, too. He stayed close to Amelia to keep her from leaning too far over the swirling water.

"Here we are, safe and sound," Sam said after they'd all made it across.

Ranger leaned in so Sam could pet him. But through all these days and miles, he kept wondering when his work would be done. When would Luke come and say, "Good job, boy!" and scratch his ears and set out his water bowl?

When would it be time to go home?

Chapter 8

THE NAMES ON THE ROCK

It was good news if you reached Independence Rock by the Fourth of July. That's what Mr. Palmer said in his guidebook. With about eight hundred miles of trail behind you, you'd be sure to make it over the mountains before the big snows came.

So there was a lot of cheering and shouting when the Abbotts' wagon train pulled into camp in front of the great granite rock. It was July 3, a full day ahead of Mr. Palmer's schedule. The Beard brothers fired their guns into the air. Mr. Harrigan played "Yankee Doodle" on his fiddle. Ma decided they'd have a special meal to celebrate.

"It looks like a big stone turtle," Sam said. "Mr. Palmer says travelers write their names on the rock. Can we go see?"

"Sure can." Pa handed Sam a tin cup of gunpowder he'd mixed with bacon grease to make a black paint. "And make your own mark as well."

"I want to do that," Lizzie said, shaking out a blanket and draping it over two barrels.

Sam turned to Sarah. "You should come, too, and write your name on the rock."

Sarah shook her head and started back toward the wagon. But Ma stepped in front of her. She tipped Sarah's chin up and looked her in the eye. "You should go. Write your parents' names if you wish. To remember them."

Sarah blinked fast and nodded. She started

after Sam and Lizzie. Then Amelia came running. "I come, too!"

Ma smiled. "Do you mind taking her with you?"

Sam sighed. "Come on, Amelia. Let's go see the big rock." Ranger snuffled along behind Amelia, just in case she thought to run off again. But she stayed close, happily holding Sam's hand on one side, Sarah's on the other.

• • •

In a few minutes, they were standing at the base of Independence Rock. Sam started to scramble up its slope, but Lizzie grabbed his sleeve.

"Look at them all." She pointed at the rock wall in front of them.

It was covered in names. Hundreds and hundreds of names. Some were full names with dates. Some just first names. They were chiseled into the rock or scratched with nails or written in looping black paint like Sam had brought. The names went on and on.

"There are so many," Lizzie whispered.

Sarah ran her hand over the inscriptions. "S. Lean. M. B. Lean." She whispered the names aloud. "They were just here a couple of months ago."

They ran their hands over the sun-warmed rock, calling out the names until Sarah gasped and jerked her hand back.

"What happened? Are you okay?" At first Sam was worried a snake had bitten her. Rattlers were common out here.

But Sarah didn't look hurt. She looked happy for the first time in weeks. "My uncle." She pointed to a name on the wall. Sam and Lizzie leaned in close to see. It was carefully written in tar, weathered some by rain and sun and wind, but as clear as could be.

Sarah pressed her hand flat against the name as if she could reach through the stone to hold his hand. "He's waiting for us in Salt Lake City. Uncle Aaron and Aunt Helen and Eliza and Martha and Abram and Mercy. They're all waiting for us to come," she whispered, and her eyes filled with tears. "Well . . . just waiting for me now, I guess." But she smiled, and Sam thought he understood why. It must have felt good to remember she still had family.

Sarah wiped her wet cheeks with her hand, and Ranger licked the salty tears from her fingers.

"You want to write your name next to your uncle's?" Sam held up the powder-and-bacon-grease mixture.

Sarah nodded and dipped her finger into

the gritty paint. Carefully, beside her uncle's name, she wrote her own.

SARAH MARGARET FERGUSON
JULY 3, 1850

Then she dipped her finger in the paint and lifted it to the rock again:

IN

Sarah paused, then looked up at Lizzie. "How do you spell *remembrance?*"

Lizzie spelled it out, and Sarah carefully marked the letters in paint on the rock.

IN REMEMBRANCE:

REBECCA ANNE FERGUSON AND
CHARLES JOSEPH FERGUSON

"Will you write yours close to mine?" Sarah asked Sam and Lizzie. She took the cup while Sam and Lizzie wrote their names on the rough surface. Lizzie added Amelia's name, too.

"You want to make your mark on the rock, Dog?" Sam grinned and knelt down. He lifted Ranger's paw, smeared it with homemade paint, and pressed it against the wall. "There! Now there's a record of your journey, too."

Ranger sniffed his paw. The bacon grease made him hungry, but he wasn't sure what to make of the black powder mixed with it. It smelled smoky and dangerous. Not good to eat.

"Let's climb to the top of the rock!" Sam said, racing up the steep slope.

"Sam, wait!" Lizzie called. "We can't take Amelia way up there. And we should get back to camp anyway."

"Oh, all right." Sam came down and followed Lizzie and Sarah, who each held one of Amelia's hands on the way back to the wagons. He leaned down and whispered to Ranger, "You and I will have to come back on our own to explore."

Chapter 9

A Secret Cave

The sun was getting ready to set after supper, but there was still plenty of light, so when Sam asked to go back to the rock, Ma nodded. "Be careful."

"I'll take Dog with me." Sam slapped his knees, and Ranger came running.

"We'll pretend we're the first ones on the trail," Sam told him as they raced toward the rock. The setting sun made it glow pinkish orange. "We can look for gold!"

Ranger galloped alongside Sam. It felt good to run with the warm wind in his fur.

When they approached the rock, Sam headed for the spot where he'd started climbing before.

But something — a vibration in the air, a sharp smell mixed with the earth and rock — made the fur on Ranger's neck prickle. Ranger barked and jumped in front of Sam to hold him back.

"Hey!" Sam stopped just as a buzzing rattle echoed off the rocks.

Sam sucked in his breath.

Curled on the rock ledge — right where Sam had been about to step — was a snake. A rattler that had to be almost four feet long. Its forked tongue darted out, tasting the air. Its tail vibrated faster, sizzling with a high-pitched warning: *Stay away!*

"Be still, Dog," Sam whispered. "Don't spook it." His voice was tight and scared.

Ranger growled low in his throat. The snake

raised its twitching tail, and another angry buzz filled the air.

The snake tasted the air again, then turned and slowly slithered away through the dust and dry grass, into a crevice.

Sam let out a rush of breath. "You are the best dog in the world!" He sank to his knees and wrapped his arms around Ranger's neck. Ranger could feel him shaking. Sam held on for a long time, and when the trembling went away, he gave Ranger one more squeeze and stood up. "Now . . . let's climb to the top!"

Sam stepped carefully from ledge to ledge, watching for snakes, but he didn't see any more. He climbed higher and higher with Ranger on his heels.

Finally, Sam stepped onto a ledge with some shade and plopped down to rest. "Let's take a break, Dog. Then we can go the rest of the way to the top."

Ranger didn't want to take a break. He thumped his paws on Sam's chest, knocked him over, and licked him all over his face. That usually got Luke moving again when he was tired.

But Sam only laughed. "I just need to catch my breath, I promise."

Ranger licked Sam's ear one more time and wandered off to sniff at a wide crack between two of the rocks. It smelled damp and cool. He pushed his nose in a little more. It was a deep crevice. Ranger barked. His bark echoed somewhere that sounded far away.

"What'd you find, Dog?" Sam leaned over him to look into the crevice. "This looks like it goes on for a bit . . ." He turned himself sideways and wiggled through until he disappeared.

Ranger barked.

"It's okay. Come on in, Dog!"

Ranger squeezed through the narrow passageway until it opened up into a cool room with rock walls. He barked again, and his woof bounced all around.

"We discovered a secret cave!" Sam looked around. When his eyes got used to the shadows, he saw writing on the walls. More names. "No . . . I guess we didn't discover it. Looks like someone else was here first."

Ranger liked the cave. The air was cool and soft in here, and he was getting tired. He turned a few times and settled on the rocky floor, head on his paws. Sam ran his hand over the names, reading them aloud.

"J. Bower was here on July 11, 1847. F. B. Chamberlain was here in 1849. Look at all the names . . . Brisbee . . . Hawk . . . Connor . . . So many people were here before us, Dog. Do you think they saw rattlesnakes or got sick or had to scare off buffalo stampedes?"

Ranger lifted his head. Luke used to talk with him like this sometimes, when they were alone in the backyard or up in Luke's bedroom. He'd talk about important things and ask questions as if Ranger were another person. Ranger could never answer, but somehow, Luke always understood he was listening. Sam seemed to understand, too.

"I wonder if they all made it to the Oregon Territory . . . or California . . . or the Great Salt Lake . . . or wherever they were going." Sam traced another name with his finger. "I hope so." Then he added, even more quietly, "I hope we all make it, too."

Ranger stood up. He walked over to Sam and nuzzled his hand.

"I'm so glad you came with us, Dog." Sam gave him a good, long scratch behind the ear.

"We should go. It will be dark soon, and Ma will have a fit if we're not back. I'll race you down!"

• • •

At the campfire that night, Sam told everyone the story of the secret cave full of names and the rattlesnake and how Ranger scared it away.

"You are a mighty fine dog," Ma told Ranger. She slipped him an extra thick slice of bacon. "Good job, boy."

There it was again. *Good job, boy*. But Luke didn't come.

Still, Ma's praise made Ranger warm inside. The greasy, salty bacon filled him up, and soon, he rested his chin on his paws and closed his eyes.

But all night long, Ranger dreamed of sharing cheeseburgers with Luke and Sadie. He imagined curling up at the foot of Luke's soft bed with the bright red comforter. He dreamed of baseballs and hot dogs and chasing squirrels around the picnic table.

When he woke, Pa and Mr. Harrigan were hitching up the oxen. It was time to start walking again.

Ranger trotted along beside Sam and Sarah. Even though they gave him extra hugs and ear scratches, he felt tired and sad. This journey seemed like it might never end. Ranger had found Amelia when she was lost. He'd warned Sam about the buffalo. He'd scared off the snake. What else was he supposed to do? There was no one lost to find. Was he going to keep walking behind this wagon forever?

Chapter 10

FAREWELLS AND SNOWBALLS

Six days after the Abbotts left Independence Rock, their wagon train got smaller. Some folks left the main trail to take a cutoff across the desert. That route could save three or four days, but it meant traveling fifty miles without water. The Beard brothers went that way. They figured anything that got them to California sooner brought them one day closer to their riches.

The Abbotts set off on the longer, safer route that led to Fort Bridger. There, Sarah would meet up with her uncle so he could take her home to the Mormon community on the Great Salt Lake.

"They say when you see it from a distance with the sun shining, it looks like a lake of gold," Sarah said as they walked behind the wagon. The hope was back in her voice, ever since she found her uncle's name on Independence Rock and wrote hers below it. Like maybe she could see a life for herself beside that sparkling lake, even though her parents were gone.

When the Abbotts arrived at the fort, Ma started asking around for Sarah's uncle right away. It wasn't long before a man hurried up to the wagon. His clothing and hair were the color of the dry grass, but his eyes were bright green. He bent down and held out his arms. "Is this our Sarah?"

Ma had wondered if Sarah would remember

her uncle. She hadn't seen him in four years, but she did. "Uncle Aaron!"

He wrapped Sarah in a hug that would have made any mama bear proud. When he finally let her go, both of their faces were streaked with tears. "We're gonna take such good care of you. Aunt Helen's got your bed all made up. Martha, Eliza, Abram, and Mercy can't wait to see you again."

Sarah smiled a little. At the campfire that night, she already seemed to be slipping away from the Abbotts and into the Clark family. She sat beside Uncle Aaron and listened to his stories about the big, salty lake.

In the morning, Sarah hugged all the Abbotts and thanked them for their kindness.

Sam pulled the three quilt squares from his pocket and unfolded them. He chose the one with the apple tree and held it out to Sarah.

"It's part of a friendship quilt my cousins made. You can keep it to remember me."

"I'll always remember you. But thank you," Sarah said. She tucked the square into her pocket and squatted down to pat Ranger. "I'm going to miss you, Dog."

Ranger nuzzled her hand. He'd miss Sarah, too, and hoped she would be all right. Seeing her small hand tucked into her uncle's big one made Ranger feel better. *Safe*, he thought. Sarah looked safe.

When Sam and his family started off on the trail that went northwest, Ranger felt an unmistakable tug to follow. Sam still needed him. The Abbotts still had a long, dangerous road ahead.

• • •

The nights had been getting colder as they went west, into the mountains. One night, it began to snow not long after they made camp. The Abbotts had to eat their stew huddled against the wagon while the wind blew snow into their faces. They all piled in the wagon to sleep that night.

In the morning, Sam woke up first. He waited outside in the snow-sparkling sunshine, hidden behind some brush and packing the snow into balls. When Lizzie climbed down with her morning frown and her hair all tangled, he launched his attack. The first snowball missed. The second hit her in the shoulder and exploded into slushy bits.

"Samuel George Abbott!" Lizzie hollered. Sam thought she'd run to Ma and get him in trouble. Instead, she bent down, gathered up a big handful of snow, and charged toward Sam's hiding spot.

He didn't have time to run. Lizzie had good

aim. She pelted him in the chest, and they both laughed.

Sam tossed a snowball in the air for Ranger, who jumped to catch it in his teeth. The snowball broke up, and clumps got stuck in the fur on Ranger's chin.

Sam laughed. "You look like you have a beard, Dog!"

Lizzie went back to the wagon to get Amelia, and they all snowballed one another while Ma and Pa laughed. By late morning, the sun had melted the snow into slush, and it was time to set out again.

In the days that followed, Sam saw more of the things he'd wondered about from his father's guidebook.

Sam drank the cold, clear water that bubbled up from the ground at Soda Springs and marveled at the spot called Steamboat Spring a little farther along the trail. It was just as Mr.

Palmer had described it: a cone about two and a half feet tall with a six-inch hole on top. Every ten seconds or so, water would come hissing and belching out the top. Sometimes it shot up higher than Sam was tall.

One evening when they made camp, the ground was covered in volcanic rocks, fragments as black as night and smooth as glass.

Another night, the mosquitoes were so thick they swirled like flakes in a snowstorm. When Ma started making bread, so many got into her bowl there was no way to pick them all out. She finally gave up and kneaded them into the dough. The bread that night was more black than white.

As they continued west, Sam started to hear his parents arguing in the wagon at night, though he didn't know why. Ranger heard it, too. Ranger could sense fear in people's voices.

He could smell it in the air, and with every passing mile, that scent grew stronger around Mrs. Abbott.

Their next stop was called Three Island Crossing. Something about it scared Ma — a lot.

Chapter 11

DANGEROUS CROSSING

It was the middle of August when the Abbotts made camp along the Snake River, getting ready to cross. That was the day Sam finally understood why his parents had been arguing.

He and Lizzie had gone to collect kindling near the river. They were walking back to the wagons when Ma's voice came drifting over the tall grass.

"It's not worth a day or two. It's not worth a hundred more days on the trail if we lose you, William!"

Lizzie motioned for Sam to stay low, and

they crouched to listen. Ranger saw a dragon-fly and started to jump at it, but Sam grabbed him around the neck and pulled him close. "Shhhh . . . Quiet, Dog."

"This is a man's decision. I've set my mind to crossing in the morning."

Ma's voice came back, just as strong. "It's a foolish man's decision. This crossing is treacherous. The number of men who have drowned —"

Sam didn't hear what she said next because Lizzie let out a great sneeze, and the conversation by the wagon either ended or became so hushed that they couldn't hear any more.

"Come on." Lizzie gathered up the sticks and dry weeds she'd set on the ground. "We'd best get this back for the fire."

"Do you think we'll cross?" Sam whispered as they started back toward the wagons.

Lizzie shrugged. "It's Pa's choice," she said. "He seems set on doing it."

"What if it's dangerous?" Sam's voice was full of worry. Ranger trotted closer and nudged his hand.

"Everything's dangerous out here," Lizzie said. "But we'll be fine. Ma frets too much."

• • •

In the morning, Pa paid some Shoshone men to ferry the wagons to the other side of the river. That's how Ma, Lizzie, Sam, Amelia, Baby Isaac, and Ranger crossed, too. They were on the far side of the river when Pa and the other men mounted their horses to drive the livestock across.

Ma stood in the mud at the edge of the river. Sam could hear her whispering prayers.

Three Island Crossing was named for the three islands in the middle of the Snake River. Travelers used two of those islands to get across. The guidebooks said getting from shore to the first island wasn't too difficult. And crossing from the first island to the second wasn't bad, either. The last crossing, from the second island to shore, was the longest and hardest — three hundred yards with a mean, fast current. Sam wasn't sure if it was last night's rain or the fact that his father had to cross soon that made the river look so swollen and fast and hungry today.

"Here they come," Lizzie said, squinting across the river.

Dr. Loring and a couple of the men from Missouri came first, driving their cattle in front of them. They crossed to the first island and then the second, just as the guidebooks directed. Their cattle were mostly across the last stretch from the second island to shore when Dr. Loring's horse reared up.

"Oh no!" Ma sucked in her breath, and they all watched as Dr. Loring clung to the reins, squeezing his saddle with his knees, trying to stay on. Sam couldn't tell what had happened to his horse, whether it stepped in a hole or got spooked by something in the water. But somehow, Dr. Loring managed to settle it down and get it moving again. When the horse climbed up the bank next to them and shook itself off, Ma let out a deep breath.

But then she tensed right back up again.

"Pa and Mr. Harrigan are starting out now." Lizzie pointed to the far shore.

Sam watched as they urged the cattle into the river and began to follow on their horses. Mr. Harrigan's horse, Bess, trotted right into the water. But old Nugget, Pa's horse, took a few steps and paused, pawing at the water, making great splashes as if this were all a game. It made Sam feel better that the horses seemed to like the river. The water wasn't deep — only just past their knees, at least for now. Sam reached into his pocket and held the quilt squares tight as Pa and Mr. Harrigan drove the cattle across to the first island.

Nugget climbed up onto the shore and shook himself.

"That wasn't so bad." Lizzie had gone over to stand by Ma.

"One down, two to go," Ma whispered. Her hands were clenched so tightly at her chin that her fingers were white.

The second part of the crossing went smoothly until the very end, when a gust of wind blew Pa's hat off his head. Mr. Harrigan leaned over to reach for it, but between the wind and the current, it was carried out of sight in seconds. Sam wondered what would happen to someone who fell into that water, but he didn't say so aloud. Ma was already humming faster than a bumblebee.

On the second island, Pa and Mr. Harrigan brought their horses close together.

Ma paced back and forth. Dr. Loring came up, still all soggy from the river, and put a hand on her shoulder. "They're going to be just fine, Mary. They were watching right close when I crossed. They'll stay clear of that trouble spot. I'm sure that's what they're talkin' about now."

"I hope you're right." Ma's voice sounded thankful but shaky. When Dr. Loring left to see to his cattle, Ranger came to stand by her. "I suppose you're looking for bacon," she said, hands on her hips. "Well, Dog . . . if they come through this safe and sound, you can have a whole slab of it. How's that?"

Ranger licked Ma's hand. Bacon was good. But mostly, he wanted Pa and Mr. Harrigan to come so everyone would stop feeling so scared and edgy. Ranger hated that prickly-neck-hair feeling. It was everywhere now, in the dust and the wind and the water. *Danger*.

Chapter 12

INTO THE RIVER

"Here they come," Lizzie said, taking a deep breath.

Pa and Mr. Harrigan drove the cattle back into the river and set out from the second island.

At first, the horses' gaits were strong and sure, but the river got deeper fast. Soon, Nugget was straining to keep his chin out of the water.

"Come on," Sam whispered. "Keep coming, Nugget." He was staring so hard at Pa and Nugget that he didn't notice what was happening to Mr. Harrigan. Bess was trying to follow

Pa and Nugget, but the current seemed to be pushing her downstream, closer and closer to the spot where Dr. Loring had trouble.

"Watch out!" Sam shouted. "It's too deep there!" But Mr. Harrigan couldn't hear him over the water. Bess was already struggling to keep her head out of the rushing river. Mr. Harrigan was close enough for Sam to see the fear on his face. He jerked the reins, but Bess was too spooked to obey. Sam could hear her whinnying and snorting. Her gait was jerky and unsure. She looked like she might rear up any second and throw Mr. Harrigan into the river, and there wasn't a thing Sam could do to stop it. So he screamed again — "It's too deep!" — even though he knew the river would swallow up his words.

At that moment, Pa turned and looked over his shoulder. He yanked his reins and turned Nugget around to go back.

"Oh, Lord," Ma whispered, clenching her hands together, shaking her head.

"It's okay, Ma." Sam tried to comfort her. "Pa's got him. Look."

Nugget was a bigger, sturdier horse. Pa rode him right up alongside Bess to keep her pushing against the river's current, and then they were moving forward again, toward shore and safety.

"See?" Sam squeezed his mother's trembling hand and looked up at her tear-streaked face. "Pa took care of it. Here they come."

"No!" Ma screamed. Sam turned in time to see Nugget going wild in the water. He didn't buck once and settle down like Dr. Loring's horse had. Nugget reared up over and over, kicking his front legs at the air as if he could fight off some invisible enemy.

Pa couldn't hold on. He lost his grip on the reins, slid off the horse, and splashed into

the river. Mr. Harrigan was right there, *should* have been close enough to grab him, but the water was frothing with stomping horse hooves and current and mud. Mr. Harrigan leaned down from his horse, hand stretched out. But Pa was already gone.

"No!" Ma wailed again. She splashed into the river up to her knees, staring out at the deep water as if she could tug Pa into shore with her eyes.

Sam couldn't breathe. He couldn't move. He could only stare as Mr. Harrigan jerked his head around, searching, looking.

Ranger ran to Sam and lifted his nose. He could smell Pa's scent in the air, along with everyone else and the horses and cattle. He smelled sage and bacon grease from breakfast and rain from last night. And above it all, he sensed cold, raw fear.

"There!" Sam hollered so hard his throat

burned. He pointed to a spot in the river, just a few feet downstream. Pa was barely keeping his head above water, trying to swim back to the horses.

Mr. Harrigan turned Bess and tried to guide her there, but it was deeper water and she was already too spooked. Pa disappeared again. When he surfaced the next time, it was farther away. Sam only saw his face for a second before the river pulled him back.

Ranger saw it, too. He'd heard this kind of shouting and seen this splashing once before, in a river in the mountains near Luke's house. "Swiftwater training," Dad had called it. Ranger and Luke had come along while Dad and the other rescue crew members practiced saving people who fell in the water. Ropes. There were lots of ropes.

Ranger broke away from Sam and raced for the wagon.

Chapter 13

GRAB THE ROPE!

Behind Ranger, the air was full of screams and cries, splashes and neighs and snorts. But Ranger ran straight for the wagon. He had seen rope earlier when Ma and Pa prepared the wagon for the ferry crossing. Where was it now?

Ranger jumped onto the tailgate and climbed between two barrels of flour. He spotted a rope that secured a trunk to the side of the wagon, but when he bit the end and tugged on it, the knots only pulled tighter.

There had to be more rope. Rope that was strong and long enough and not all tied up to something. Ranger jumped over a wooden trunk and sniffed at the tools that hung along the sides of the wagon. Iron. Steel. Rust.

Finally, he smelled something else — fiber and sweat — and found a thick coil of rope tucked behind a crate of dried fruit. Ranger clamped his teeth on the rope and tugged as hard as he could. The rope came loose. Ranger took the end in his mouth, leaped from the wagon, and ran for the riverbank.

Lizzie held Isaac in her arms and clutched Amelia's hand. Sam was with Ma, practically holding her up as they shouted to Mr. Harrigan over the raging water. Dr. Loring called to the other men for help.

Ranger raced up to Sam and thrust the rope at his hands.

"You brought rope!" Sam grabbed it, but Ranger tugged one end back and plunged into the water. With the rope in his teeth, he swam past Mr. Harrigan and Bess, toward the place where he'd last seen Pa.

The air was wet and full of smells — horse sweat and river plants and fish. Ranger caught the scent of death, too, rising up from the water. There were bodies down there. But Pa was still alive. Ranger could smell him. His scent got stronger as Ranger let the river carry him farther downstream.

But there was no sign of Pa in the water, and Ranger was getting tired.

The current fought against him. It tugged at his rope and whipped a loop around his legs. He had to kick them free to keep swimming. It got harder and harder to keep his head out of the water so he could see.

Ranger knew he couldn't last much longer. He'd have to let go of the rope and swim to shore. He'd have to rest and breathe and try again. But would Pa's alive-and-fighting smell still be strong then?

The rope jerked tight. Ranger almost lost it, but he clamped his teeth down hard and held on. Ranger felt the water rushing past him; he had run out of rope. Sam held tight to the other end on the bank. Ranger couldn't go any farther without letting go.

Ranger struggled to lift his head. He couldn't see Sam or Mr. Harrigan anymore, but he caught a splash in the water just a dog's length or two away. A hand shot out of the waves, flailing at the air, grabbing at nothing. Then, for a flash of a moment, Ranger saw Pa's terrified face, gasping for breath before he was swept underwater again.

Ranger kicked as hard as he could, back upstream. He had to battle the current to move even the tiniest bit. The rope scratched his mouth and his tongue. The river slapped at his face, but Ranger swam as hard as he could. Finally, his paw touched something solid. The rough, wet fabric of Pa's shirt.

Pa's arm jerked away, and then his head popped out of the water. He coughed, taking in great, desperate gulps of air. His arms flopped and slapped at the river as he tried to stay afloat.

The rope! Ranger swam closer. *Here!* he thought. *Take it!*

In the swiftwater training with Dad and Luke, the person had taken the rope right away. Ranger had been watching from the boat. The rope came and the person grabbed it and got saved. But this was different. Training hadn't smelled like this — like fear and panic and coughed-up river water.

Ranger swam right up beside Pa, kicked him in the shoulder, and poked him in the ear with his nose. Finally, Pa's eyes focused on the dog and then — *Yes!* — he lunged at the rope.

Sam must have seen Pa's hand close around it because right away, the rope pulled tight again. Ranger wasn't sure Pa was strong enough to keep hanging on, so he tried to swim beside him. But Ranger was exhausted, and the current was strong. It was starting to pull him away from Pa, away from the rope and safety. Pa flung an arm around Ranger and held him tight until they finally saw Sam tugging on that rope.

Sam cried when he finally saw his pa. He and Dr. Loring pulled Pa and Ranger all the way into shore, until the water was shallow

enough for Pa to crawl. Then they splashed out to help him onto dry land.

Pa coughed up some water, then flopped onto his back and looked up at the sky.

Ranger stood in the mud and looked up, too. It felt like something should happen. He'd rescued Pa. Would Luke come and take him home now? But when he heard the words "Good job," it was Sam's voice — not Luke's.

"You're such a good boy." Sam put his face close to Ranger's. "I love you, Dog."

Ranger loved Sam, too.

But he was still all wet. Ranger shook water onto Sam, and everyone laughed. Nothing had ever sounded so good.

• • •

Later, when all the clothes were hung up to dry, Ma gave Ranger that slab of bacon she'd promised him. "You deserve that and more,

Dog." She patted him on the head, and Ranger wolfed down the meat.

But Sam wasn't eating. Ma raised her eyebrows. "Did all that adventure steal away your appetite?"

Sam shrugged. He'd been quiet all night, and Ranger thought he felt warm. Maybe too warm. Ranger sniffed at Sam's temple and whined.

Ma squatted down next to Sam and put her hand to his forehead. Ranger felt the air change again. The smell of fear was back even before it crackled out in Ma's voice. "Get the medicine chest, Lizzie. He's burning up."

Chapter 14

FEVER DREAMS

Sam didn't eat anything at supper, or at breakfast the next morning. Ma and Pa settled him in some blankets piled on a trunk in the wagon, and he rode there for the next three days. Ranger walked alongside Lizzie and Amelia, but every time the wagon stopped, he leaped onto the back and found his way back to Sam.

Dr. Loring came by at the end of every day on the trail. He cut Sam's arm so the bad blood could drain out, but Sam still shivered under his scratchy wool blanket.

Ma was afraid he had cholera like Sarah's

mother and father. But Dr. Loring pointed to the red spots spreading from Sam's wrists and ankles, right up his arms and legs. "Mountain fever," he said, studying the rash. "It's danger-ous, but I think he'll make it."

On the morning of the fourth day, Sam's skin wasn't so hot. He even got up and walked behind the wagon for a bit. But when night fell, the fever came back. And it was worse. Much worse. Sam was shaking his head and twitching his limbs as if some invisible wolf had gotten hold of him.

Dr. Loring came and gave Sam some medi-cine, but he spit it back up. Dr. Loring turned to Ma and shook his head. "The second phase is usually worse than the first. All we can do is pray."

"Come on, Dog, get down!" Lizzie called. But Ranger wouldn't leave Sam's side. When Luke was sick last year, Ranger had stayed with him the whole time, sleeping beside him in bed. Luke had gotten better. Sam would, too. He had to, didn't he?

Days passed, but Sam didn't improve. When Sam shivered, Ranger curled up close to him. When Sam cried out, Ranger licked his hand. Mostly, Ranger sat beside him, keeping watch.

Ranger heard Lizzie say they were almost to the Oregon Territory. Any day, Uncle Thomas would come down the river to meet them and see them back to the farm. Sam *had* to get better; he'd waited so long to see this new country.

Ranger ate the scraps that were offered at night, but nothing tasted the same when Sam wasn't eating. The days blurred together until finally, Ranger woke one morning to find Sam sitting up beside him, blinking into the rising sun.

"Good morning, Dog. I'm thirsty. And hungry, I think." Ranger wasn't sure what Sam

wanted, but he understood the most important thing. Sam was back.

Ranger barked, and Ma came running. She
just about smothered Sam in hugs and corn
bread. When Sam first stood up, his legs were
as wobbly as a newborn colt's, but the color
was coming back to his cheeks.

At the end of the day, a wagon appeared on
the trail, coming from the other direction. Ma
raised her hand to shade her eyes from the
sun. "William! I do believe that's your brother's team!"

Lizzie gathered her skirts in her arms and
broke into a run. Even though he was still
weak, Sam took Amelia's hand and followed.
"Uncle Thomas!"

The wagon stopped alongside the trail. A
sturdy-looking man jumped down from his
horse and came running with a floppy-eared
dog alongside him. Uncle Thomas looked a

little older than Pa, with the same scruffy red hair and green eyes. He rushed up to the Abbotts' wagon, hugging Ma and fussing over the baby and telling Amelia how grown up she was. The dog nearly knocked Amelia off her feet.

"Finnegan!" Uncle Thomas called, and the dog barked. "Leave that little miss alone." Finnegan jumped up on Sam and nuzzled his hand.

"Does Finnegan live on the farm?" Sam asked.

Uncle Thomas nodded. "He'll wake you up every morning, I promise."

"Did you hear that, Dog?" Sam turned to the wagon, where Ranger had been standing, watching.

Ranger barked and tipped his head. But he stayed by the wagon. He had heard Uncle Thomas. He'd heard Sam. And now he heard something else.

A high-pitched humming, coming from inside the wagon. It was getting louder and louder.

Ranger hopped up on the tailgate and found it right away. The metal box from the garden at home was there, where Ma had tucked it next to the tools on that first day, way back in the dusty square. The box was vibrating urgently.

Ranger had done a good job. Now it was time to go home.

Ranger grabbed the leather strap with his teeth, dragged it to the wagon's tailgate, and jumped down. Sam was watching him. Ranger knew he couldn't leave without saying good-bye.

Everyone was getting ready to start off again, to finish the journey. The metal box was humming so loud it seemed to be shaking the whole earth. But Ranger set it down in the dirt, ran to Sam, and licked his hand.

"Dog, this is Finnegan," Sam said, squatting to introduce them. Finnegan nuzzled Sam's ear, then turned to look at Ranger curiously. "Who are you?" the other dog seemed to ask. Finnegan sniffed Ranger as if he didn't quite belong.

"We're going home now," Sam said, "to the farm."

Ranger sniffed Finnegan. He was a good dog. He'd take care of Sam.

"Sam, come along," Pa called. "We need to make ten more miles before dark."

Ranger licked Sam's hand once more and turned away.

"Where you going, Dog?" Sam looked confused. He stood up, and one of the quilt squares fluttered down from his pocket. "Aren't you coming?"

Ranger sniffed the square, then picked it up carefully in his teeth.

"You want to carry that for me? Here . . ."

Sam took the bit of fabric and tucked it under Ranger's collar. "All set now?"

"Let's go, son!" Pa called. "That dog will follow if he wants to. We need to get moving."

But Sam didn't move. He watched Ranger trot back to the first aid kit and sit down. Finally, Sam nodded as if he understood. "Thanks, Dog," he said quietly.

But Ranger heard. Even over the humming that threatened to swallow him up. He watched Sam run to catch up with Lizzie and Finnegan and the wagon. When Ranger nuzzled the dusty leather strap over his head, the humming drowned out all the sounds of the trail — the snorting and shouting, the clomping of oxen hooves, and the neighing of horses.

Ranger saw a pinprick of white light that grew bigger and bigger until it swallowed up the Oregon sun and Ranger had to close his eyes. When he opened them, there was a squirrel.

Chapter 15

HOME!

The squirrel crouched at the bottom of the oak tree, its muscles twitching as if it might race back up into the leaves any second.

Ranger sniffed the air. He smelled squirrel. He smelled the fresh-grass-and-gasoline twang of Dad's lawn mower. He smelled Luke and Sadie and pizza, and somewhere, still buried in the garden dirt, a bone from a long-ago steak.

The squirrel twitched again. Instead of running up the tree, it took off toward the picnic table, and before Ranger could even think, he was chasing it, legs flying behind him, ears perked up, nose sniffing ahead of him. *Squirrel!*

They raced three times around the picnic table, through Mom's flowers, across the garden, and then *zip!* The squirrel raced up the oak tree and vanished into the shaking leaves above.

"Poor Ranger. Another one got away. Want a treat, boy?"

Ranger turned and saw Luke open the kitchen door. He bent down and held out his hand with a half slice of bacon in his open palm.

Ranger rushed up to him, panting, and gobbled it up. *Bacon!*

Home bacon!

Ranger followed Luke inside to the mudroom, still licking grease from his muzzle.

"What's that?" Luke reached for the first aid kit that hung around Ranger's neck.

Ranger stood still while Luke lifted the strap and studied the rusty tin box. Then he noticed the quilt square and slipped it from under Ranger's collar. "Did you dig all this up in the garden? That's pretty cool. Let's show Mom." He started to walk off. Without thinking, Ranger barked.

Luke turned, his eyes wide. "What?"

Ranger trotted up to Luke and carefully took the leather strap and quilt square in his teeth. He tugged until Luke let go. "Okay, fine. You found the stuff. It's all yours. Whatcha gonna do with it?"

Ranger carried it to his dog bed.

Luke laughed. "I guess that's a good place to keep your treasures. Good job! You're a good boy, Ranger!" He scratched Ranger's ear.

Ranger leaned in and wagged his tail. He'd waited so long to hear those words.

When Luke left, Ranger settled into his dog bed. He was tired. But before he went to sleep, he nuzzled the first aid kit. It was quiet now. The humming had stopped.

Ranger poked at the kit with his nose until it was tucked into the folds of his blanket. Then he curled up and gave the quilt square a good, long sniff. Sam's scent still clung to the fabric. Ranger could smell Ma, too — her mix of wildflowers and worry. And Lizzie and Amelia and trail bacon and oxen.

But mostly Sam.

Somehow, Ranger knew Sam was home now, too.

AUTHOR'S NOTE

Imagine saying good-bye to your house, almost all of your friends and extended family, and most of your possessions. Imagine leaving everything you know to begin a long, long journey to a new home in a place you've never seen. The decision to set out on the Oregon Trail must have been a difficult one to make, but thousands of families like the Abbotts made that choice in the mid-1800s.

Sam and his family are fictional, but their story is inspired by the diaries and journals of many real-life people who wrote a little bit each night as they traveled west on the overland trails that led not only to the Oregon Territory but also to California and the Great Salt Lake. The trip usually took about five months. That's if everything went well. Bad weather, disease, and trouble with livestock could all slow down the pace of travel.

Like Sam's family, many people traveled in mixed groups, often with different destinations. In the earliest days of the trail, many families were heading to the Oregon Territory for farmland. Starting in 1846, they were joined by Mormons like Sarah's family, who were bound for the Great Salt Lake area to escape religious persecution. When gold was discovered in California in 1849, another group of travelers headed west. The Beard brothers are fictional, but they represent the thousands of men — and some women, too — who left their homes to search for fortune in the California Gold Rush.

Many people started their journeys in one of the towns known as jumping-off points. While Sam's family set off from Independence, Missouri, others chose to leave from St. Joseph, Missouri, or Council Bluffs, Iowa. Wherever the trip started, the preparations looked much the same. Most families used a guidebook like the one the Abbotts carry. Theirs was written by Joel Palmer, who traveled west in 1845 and 1846. These guidebooks suggested routes and strategies. They also gave lists of needed supplies and directions for setting up a wagon.

Palmer and other real-life emigrants wrote about lots of animals in their journals. They described prairie dog towns and buffalo stampedes. They wrote about gathering buffalo dung for fuel, circling wagons at night, and listening to the wolves howl. The snowball fight Sam's family has in this book is based on one that Margaret Frink described in her 1850 trail diary as she camped near the Platte River in June:

> At dark, while I was cooking supper, a heavy storm of wind and snow came up. There was no shelter, and we ate our supper while it was snowing and blowing. During the night, the men took turns guarding the horses in the snow, Mr. Frink being with them part of the time.
>
> Tuesday, June 18. This was a bright June morning. We snowballed each other till ten o'clock, when the sun got too warm for the snow to remain.
>
> (Kenneth L. Holmes, ed. *Covered Wagon Women, Volume 2: Diaries and Letters from the Western Trails, 1850* [Lincoln: University of Nebraska Press, 1996])

Diseases were a constant worry on the trail. The cholera that leaves Sarah an orphan and the mountain fever that nearly kills Sam are just two examples. Today, historians and scientists understand the causes for those illnesses, which are no longer the great threat they were in the 1850s. Today's experts know that unsanitary conditions and contaminated drinking water contributed to the cholera epidemic. They believe tick bites were most likely the cause of one kind of "mountain fever," which we now know as Rocky Mountain spotted fever.

While some pioneer families worried about encounters with Native Americans along the trail, most who traveled around 1850 had experiences similar to the Abbotts. More than twenty different tribes lived and passed through the areas around the Oregon Trail. The Sioux and Shoshone who helped Sam's family are frequently mentioned in real historical diaries from this time period. They traded with travelers, served as guides, and assisted with river crossings. In the later days of emigration, there was more tension. Violence between the groups became more common, especially after the U.S. government began sending more soldiers west and some military commanders broke treaties that had been made with the tribes.

In researching Ranger and Sam's adventure, I became immersed in diaries, journals, trail guides, maps, and artifacts. The National Frontier Trails Museum and Merrill J. Mattes Research Library in Independence, Missouri, served as amazing time machines, plunging me back to the days of the Oregon Trail.

One of the people I met in those faded journals was Lizzie Charleton, a real-life teenager who traveled west with her family in 1866. Sam's ever-complaining older sister was inspired by the real Lizzie's journals.

April the 19th last night it rained & made the roads so muddy that we did not start until noon we travailed 14 miles to day & it rained all day & is so cold we like to freeze to death

April the 20th This morning it is still cold enough for winter we travailed until 2 o clock today & it was so disagreeable & cold we had to stop the rest of the day

May the 14th Camped for to night on the bank of Platte River it looks verry much like we might have a storm to night came 18 miles to day through sand & mud holes till there is no name for it & I am vary tired a walking

I owe many thanks to those who helped me on my time-traveling journey, especially Richard Edwards of the National Frontier Trails Museum, who introduced me to Lizzie via her diary, and Patrick Sutton from the Independence Rock State Historic Site, who told me all about Sam and Ranger's "secret cave" and sent me photographs of the names recorded on the rocks inside.

Ranger was inspired by the stories of many real-life search-and-rescue dogs. When I was doing research for the Ranger in Time series, I spent time with Oakland and Easton, who are part of the Champlain Valley K-9 Unit, and their handlers, Shannon Bresett and Kelly Gidman.

Oakland is a German shepherd who is an air scent dog. Even though I'd read so much about these dogs, I was amazed by how focused and excited he was to do his work.

Easton is a chocolate Lab who uses both air scenting and ground tracking to find people. He also made quick work of a couple challenges we set up to practice "finding victims" in the Adirondack woods. Both dogs found their target scents in the air and followed them to the fallen trees and brush piles where their "scent objects" were hiding. I was one of those scent objects. I had run through a field into thick brush and crouched behind a big old log. I thought I was hidden well, but Easton found me in seconds by following my scent. Here's a picture of us celebrating his find:

Like Ranger, these dogs are excited to do their work. They look forward to a reward after a job well done. Their handlers lavish them with lots of petting and praise — "Good dog! Good job!" — followed by a drink of water. Then, like Ranger, they finally get to go home.

FURTHER READING

Daily Life in a Covered Wagon by Paul Erickson (Puffin, 1997)

If You Traveled West in a Covered Wagon by Ellen Levine (Scholastic, 1992)

Sniffer Dogs: How Dogs (and Their Noses) Save the World by Nancy Castaldo (Houghton Mifflin/ Harcourt, 2014)

Words West: Voices of Young Pioneers by Ginger Wadsworth (Clarion Books, 2003)

SOURCES

Butruille, Susan G. *Women's Voices from the Oregon Trail: The Times That Tried Women's Souls, and a Guide to Women's History along the Oregon Trail.* Boise, ID: Tamarack, 1993.

Faragher, John Mack. *Women and Men on the Overland Trail*. New Haven, CT: Yale University Press, 2001.

Frémont, John Charles. *The Expeditions of John Charles Frémont*. Edited by Donald Jackson and Mary Lee Spence. Urbana: University of Illinois, 1970.

Hewitt, James, ed. *Eye-witnesses to Wagon Trains West*. New York: Scribner, 1973.

Hileman, Levida. *In Tar and Paint and Stone: The Inscriptions at Independence Rock and Devil's Gate*. Glendo, WY: High Plains Press, 2001.

Holmes, Kenneth L., ed. *Best of Covered Wagon Women*. Norman: University of Oklahoma Press, 2008.

Lienhard, Heinrich. *From St. Louis to Sutter's Fort, 1846*. Translated and edited by Erwin G. Gudde and Elisabeth K. Gudde. Norman: University of Oklahoma Press, 1961.

Marcy, Randolph Barnes. *The Prairie Traveler: A*

Hand-book for Overland Expeditions. New York: Harper & Brothers, 1861.

Mattes, Merrill J. *The Great Platte River Road: The Covered Wagon Mainline via Fort Kearny to Fort Laramie*. Lincoln: Nebraska State Historical Society, 1969.

Meldahl, Keith Heyer. *Hard Road West: History and Geology along the Gold Rush Trail*. Chicago: University of Chicago Press, 2007.

Morgan, Dale L. *Overland in 1846: Diaries and Letters of the California-Oregon Trail*. Georgetown, CA: Talisman Press, 1963.

Palmer, Joel. *Journal of Travels Over the Oregon Trail in 1845*. Portland: Oregon Historical Society Press, 1993.

Peters, Harold J., ed. *Seven Months to Oregon: 1853, Diaries, Letters and Reminiscent Accounts*. Tooele, UT: Patrice Press, 2008.

Schlissel, Lillian. *Women's Diaries of the Westward Journey*. New York: Schocken Books, 1982.

Thwaites, Reuben Gold. *Early Western Travels 1748–1846: A Series of Annotated Reprints of Some of the Best and Rarest Contemporary Volumes of Travel, Descriptive of the Aborigines and Social and Economic Conditions in the Middle and Far West, During the Period of Early American Settlement.* New York: AMS, 1966.

Unruh, John D., Jr. *The Plains Across: The Overland Emigrants and the Trans-Mississippi West, 1840–60.* Urbana: University of Illinois Press, 1979.

ABOUT THE AUTHOR

Kate Messner is the author of *The Brilliant Fall of Gianna Z.*, recipient of the E. B. White Read Aloud Award for Older Readers; *Capture the Flag*, a Crystal Kite Award winner; *Over and Under the Snow*, a *New York Times* Notable Children's Book; and the Marty McGuire chapter book series. A former middle-school English teacher, Kate lives on Lake Champlain with her family and loves reading, walking in the woods, and traveling. Visit her online at www.katemessner.com.

DON'T MISS RANGER'S NEXT ADVENTURE . . . IN ANCIENT ROME!

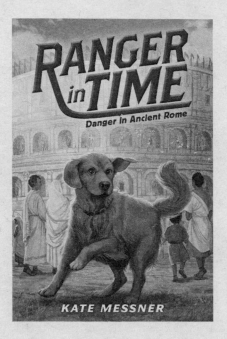

Ranger travels to the time of gladiator fights and wild animal hunts at the Colosseum, where he rescues a young boy from a runaway lion. But for gladiators and the servants who help to run the games, there's no escape from Emperor Domitian's brutal world of the arena . . . or is there?